The Medieval Household

by Jean Ellenby
illustrated by Belinda Harrould

Produced by Dinosaur Publications for
Cambridge University Press

Cambridge
New York   New Rochelle
Melbourne   Sydney

Published by the Press Syndicate of the University of Cambridge
The Pitt Building, Trumpington Street, Cambridge CB2 1RP
32 East 57th Street, New York, NY 10022, USA
10 Stamford Road, Oakleigh, Melbourne 3166, Australia

First published 1986
Reprinted 1987

Printed in Great Britain by Frank Peters (Printers) Ltd

ISBN 0 521 301181 hard cover
ISBN 0 521 317487 paperback

The Middle Ages

In a single day in 1066, the Battle of Hastings was fought and lost. King Harold of the Saxons was killed when an arrow pierced his eye, and his army was defeated. William of Normandy – or William the Conqueror as he was called – became King of England.

King William declared that even though the whole of England belonged to him, his barons and knights could have some land because he could not look after it all himself. He gave them manors – usually a large house and its surrounding village. In return, each knight had to pay rent and promise to raise men who he would lead to battle in the King's Army whenever they were needed. These lords of the manor kept some of the land for themselves, and let the villagers, or villeins, keep their homes and strips of ground in exchange for crops and work. Some paid rent, but most villeins had to work for several days every week tending the lord's crops. This was called the feudal system and it continued in Britain for several hundred years. The system did not break down until after the years of the Black Death (between 1348 and 1351) when about a third of the population died.

The Middle Ages was a long period of gradual change, lasting for nearly five hundred years. Although there was constant warfare with France, Scotland and Wales and even between the supporters of the families of York and Lancaster in the Wars of the Roses, life at home was very settled and secure. Each village was an isolated community where people lived and worked for the whole of their lives. Roads were just rutted tracks, so news and ideas travelled very slowly. In any case most people were far too busy struggling to grow enough food to be interested in what was happening outside their village.

Villages

England at this time was mostly covered in forest or
heath, with small villages in the scattered clearings where
trees had been felled. In each village the cottages were
clustered around the church. Fifty dwellings made a large
settlement – about the size of a short street today. Most
thatched cottages were made of a wooden frame, roughly
pegged together, with walls of mud, or perhaps wattle
and daub – a thick paste of clay and straw smeared over a
mesh woven of springy twigs. Some dwellings had two
curved timbers at each end fastened together in pairs at
the top, making the shape of wishbones. These were
called cruck cottages and were much sturdier than the
others.

Each home had a croft, a small patch of soil where the family planted onions, cabbages and peas for the cooking pot. A few scrawny chickens pecked hopefully for scraps and a puny pig or two snuffled around, wandering in and out of the dwelling. The rest of the cleared land around the village was divided into a great meadow for hay and three large open fields where crops were grown. Each year, while one field was planted with wheat for bread, another was sown with barley for ale, oats for the cattle and perhaps some beans to be dried and stored for the household. The third field would lie empty. Cattle were put out to graze on the weeds in this fallow field and their dung added a rich manure to the soil. The following year a different field would lie fallow and in this way the crops were rotated between the three fields and the soil remained fresh and fertile.

Manor houses

In the manor house lived the lord, his family and all his servants. It was much larger than the cottages of the peasants, but was only slightly more comfortable. It had one towering room, or great hall, with a small room (called the solar) divided off at one end. This was where the lord and his lady slept. Because of the risk of fire, the kitchen was usually quite separate from the rest of the house. This meant that when the food reached the table in the hall it was often tepid and spoilt.

To make them safer from attack, some halls had their only entrance on the first floor, reached by an outside staircase. Underneath was the arched storeroom where tools and grain were kept. The thick walls were usually made of local stone, though some manor houses were made of wooden beams with wattle and daub packed between the posts. Heavy rafters supported a thatched or stone-tiled roof. All the timber needed for the house was split from the trunks of huge oak trees felled in the nearby forests.

Whether the manor house was built in a beautiful valley or on a bleak hillside it made no difference to the size of the windows. They were always narrow slits which were wider on the inside. The wind whistling through these 'wind-eyes' gave them their name. They did let a little light into the hall, but at night were covered over with wooden shutters. Glass was a rare luxury in the Middle Ages and anyone rich enough to have glass window panes always removed them if they left the house. Sometimes thin transparent layers were peeled or shaved from the horns of cattle and glued into a lattice frame; or pieces of oiled linen, which allowed a faint light to filter through, were used.

In the main hall there was a stone hearth in the centre of the floor. Smoke curled and twisted its way up to a hole in the roof, which was shielded by a louver to stop the rain from pouring in and putting out the fire. Towards the end of the period, houses had the fireplace at the side of the room with a flue in the wall to allow the smoke to escape.

Farming

The rough heathland round the edge of the village was common land, used by everyone as pasture. Here cattle grazed among noisy geese and bleating sheep. In autumn the lean pigs were allowed to roam the forests, growing a little fatter by grubbing out fallen acorns. When they were killed, the meat was smoked over the wood fire to become bacon. People knew nothing about growing root vegetables for winter fodder, so as soon as the first frosts came, most of the cattle were slaughtered. Then the carcasses had to be cut up and salted to stop the meat from going rotten.

Most of the villagers could only work on their own strips for three days a week. Sunday was a day of rest, although sometimes at harvest time this rule was broken – with the priest's permission. For the remaining three days the villagers had to work on the land surrounding the manor house – the lord's 'demesne'. There were many jobs to do – ploughing, sowing and harrowing, weeding, harvesting and threshing, and even making cider or mending the roof. Although it was sometimes a nuisance to have to stop their own work and help on the demesne, it did mean that the villagers were secure in their homes because the lord of the manor needed his villeins. He simply could not farm all his land by himself.

The villagers had to work hard on the land and every family had several strips scattered about in the three unfenced fields. This made sure that everyone had an equal share of the rich and the stony soil. The strips were ploughed by oxen which ambled along, slowly and lazily. The length of the strip became fixed by the distance the oxen would pull the plough before pausing for a rest.

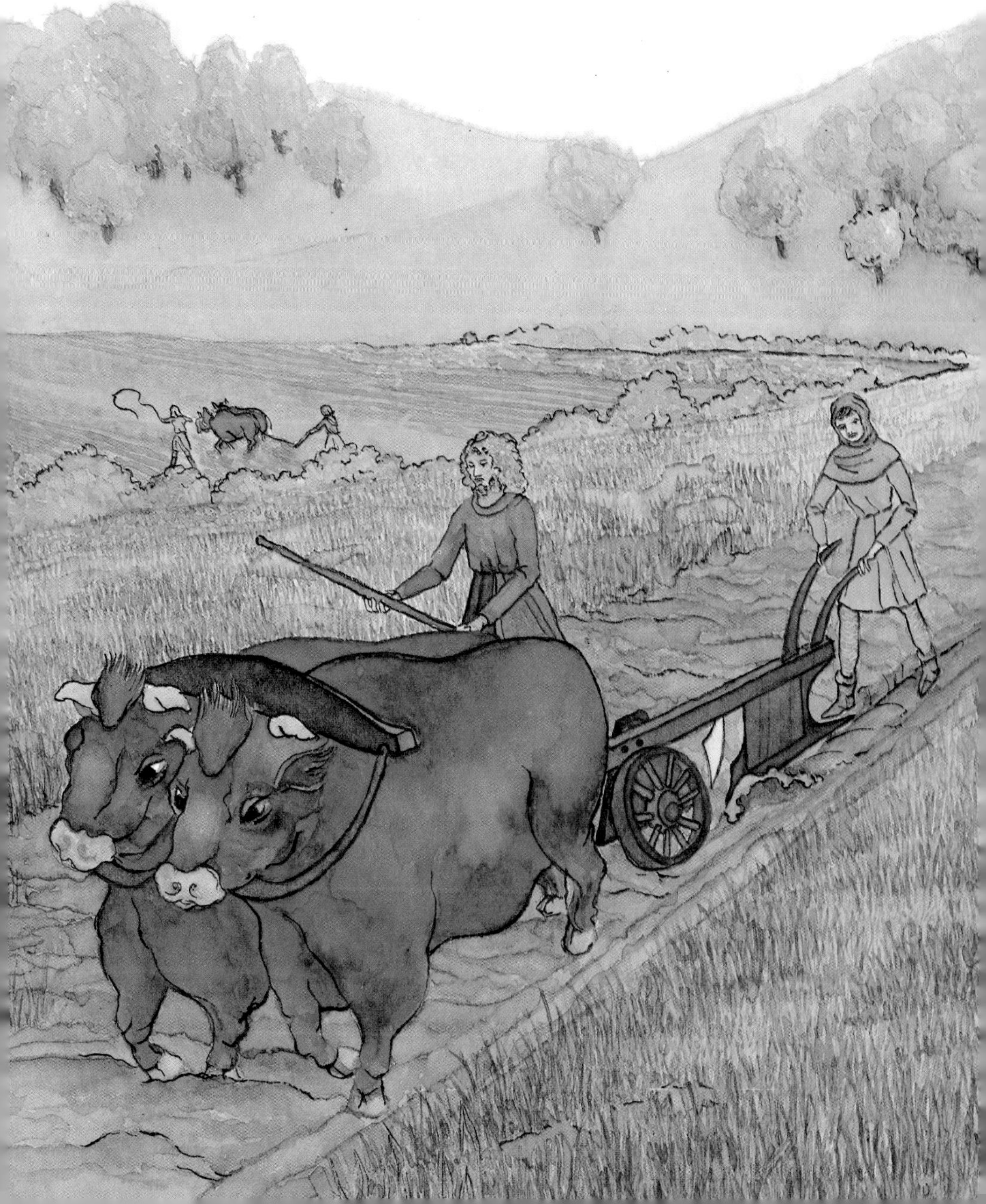

The lord of the manor

The lord of the manor had to pay his rent and give service to the King, so he had to make sure that the villeins did not shirk their duties. A bailiff and a reeve helped him in this task. The bailiff checked that each villein did his feudal duties by working the correct number of days on the lord's demesne and paid his dues: 'One fat hen at Christmas, six fresh eggs every week and a healthy piglet once a year', was a typical agreement.

The reeve looked after the work out of doors. He decided which crops should be grown in the fields, and when they should be planted and harvested. Every day he tramped around the manor watching carefully, and a blast on his horn announced the start or finish of a rest for bread and ale.

By law, all the corn in the village had to be ground at the mill owned by the lord of the manor. The villeins resented this bitterly because in exchange they had to give the lord some of their flour. They often mistrusted the miller because they suspected he sometimes swopped the grain for a poorer quality and gave them short measure, as well!

Every six weeks the lord was the chief judge at the manor court held in the great hall, where dues were paid and all complaints heard. The entire village attended and watched with horror or glee as tremendous arguments took place and wrong-doers were fined. Although serious crimes, like theft or murder, were taken to a higher court, offences like dues not paid, work not done on the demesne, or the felling of trees without permission, were all brought to the attention of the lord by the bailiff or reeve. Disagreements between neighbours over straying cattle or moving boundary stones, were sorted out and heavy fines were given for occasional violent squabbles which had ended up with a split lip or bloody nose.

Hunting, fishing and falconing

One of the great joys of living in a country practically covered in woodland was hunting the wild animals which sheltered among the trees. The Medieval monarchs loved this sport and declared many areas Royal Forests where nobody could hunt without their permission.

The lord of the manor often enjoyed catching hares with his dogs, a sport called hare coursing, but sometimes the baron invited him and other local lords to join a hunting party in the forest. Mounted on horses, they galloped eagerly into the woods, following the hounds who had scented a stag. Their servants followed breathlessly on foot, desperately trying to keep up with the hunt. Naturally many villagers could not resist a stealthy expedition after dark to try and shoot a deer with bows and arrows, but the punishments for poaching were very severe. For wounding a deer a man could have his hand or ear chopped off, and for killing a deer the offender was hanged. However, there was a law that if an animal strayed out of the forest it was no longer protected, and when this happened the entire village gave chase, anxious for some fun and a piece of tasty venison instead of the usual vegetable soup or scrawny rabbit.

The lord owned all the fishing rights on the manor and often some member of his household would sit on the river bank catching fresh pike, carp or perch to make a change from supper. Eels were caught too – trapped in long wicker baskets wedged in the fast flowing waters of the mill race.

Most wealthy manor houses had a falconer. It was his job to care for the hawks and falcons, and skilfully train them to hunt rabbits, duck and other wild birds. Both lords and their ladies took part in this sport, wearing thick leather gloves to protect themselves from the vicious claws of the birds. The hawk, with a fancy leather hood covering its face, perched on the hunter's wrist until the prey was sighted. Quickly, the hood was removed, and away flew the hawk to swoop on its victim which it instantly killed. A dog was sent to collect the dead game while the hawk was lured back to its perch.

Furniture

Eating and sleeping, laughing and squabbling, dancing
and kissing – all took place in the great hall. There was
very little furniture. Tables were plain wooden boards,
supported on trestles. After meals, they were taken apart
and propped against the walls to make more room for
work or for fun and games. People sat on long benches
made from planks, nailed or fastened together with
wooden pegs – screws had not yet been invented.

The lord and his lady, and sometimes an important
visitor, sat on the only chairs. These were often fixed to
the wall at the top end of the hall. They were carved from
wood and had sturdy arms and a high back. The seat was
actually a large box, sometimes used as a chest, and they
were very hard and uncomfortable. However, it was a
sign of the owner's importance to use a chair and this is
why nowadays the person in charge of the meeting is said
to 'take the chair', because years ago nobody else would
have had one.

Each family had an oak chest to hold their few clothes
and treasures. It was often brightly painted and fastened
with a heavy padlock. Rich lords had several chests,
including an iron strong-box for storing precious
documents and money. There were no banks, so the
safety of his valuables was the lord's responsibility.

At night, most of the household wrapped themselves in
their cloaks and lay down on the straw beside the fire to
sleep. The only bed was a magnificent, carved four-poster
belonging to the lord of the manor. Here he and his lady
slept in linen sheets with woollen blankets and perhaps a
fur cover. Before solars or private rooms became common
the bed was placed at one end of the hall. Heavy curtains
hung from the frame and were closed to keep out the
draughts and gave some privacy from the rest of the
household. On cold winter mornings this was the
warmest place to be, and it was quite usual for a lord to
remain tucked up in bed while he listened to the latest
gossip brought by a passing traveller.

The daily round

A medieval household would be up at the crack of dawn so as not to waste precious daylight hours, especially in winter when there was very little time to get the chores finished. Although there were wax candles and rush tapers, they gave out a weak, fluttering light which scarcely reached the dark corners or the lofty ceiling of the hall. Candles were also very costly so most people went to bed as soon as it became dark. It was only the lord who could afford to stay up late – going to bed after 8 o'clock was thought to be very extravagant!

Servants had to draw all the water for the household from an outside well. The water was often dirty and sometimes even a dead mouse or frog was hauled up in a bucket. Clothes were very rarely changed, but occasionally they were washed in the river – first pounded on the bank with a flat stick to beat out all the dirt and then rinsed in the cold and often muddy water.

Ladies washed their faces and hands indoors, but the men of the household had to splash themselves with cold water from a trough in the yard. To have a bath was a very rare treat. Some rich houses had a wooden bath tub but, because filling it with hot water was such a chore, it was only used three or four times a year. Young men found the best way of bathing was to strip off all their clothes and jump into the common pool at the river. But as the church began to disapprove of these merry bathing parties they stopped and people stayed dirty instead.

There were no water closets at this time. Most people used earth closets in the yard of the manor house. The lord and his family used these, and so did female servants, but male servants used the fields or perhaps squatted behind a nearby bush! Some large manor houses had special rooms called latrines, with a wooden seat over a hole which let straight into the moat or a cesspool. The stench rising from these open sewers was appalling – especially on a warm summer's day.

Kitchens

The master cook was a very important person in the manor household. He was in charge of a large staff, from the skilled pastry chef to the boy who worked the bellows to keep the fires roaring. The master cook always carried a long wooden spoon with him – to dip into soups and sauces for a stir and a taste, or to wallop the backside of a lazy servant!

Because so many people lived and ate at the manor house the kitchens were enormous and usually had two or three fires. Over one hung a pan of water – the only way that water could be heated in those days. Over another simmered a huge cauldron of bean or pea soup, strongly flavoured with onions and garlic and lots of garden herbs. In the summer a whole side of freshly-killed ox, or a few piglets or chickens might be stuck on a spit. It was the duty of a young boy to turn the spit and make sure the meat roasted evenly. In winter the only fresh meat was wild game from the forests or pigeons from the lord's dovecote. The villagers got very upset about these fat pigeons because they gobbled up the grain growing in the fields. When there was no fresh meat or fish, some salt pork or beef was boiled in a pot for hours with generous pinches, or even handfuls, of exotic spices to try and hide the foul taste of the stale meat. Sometimes it was so old and rotten that maggots crawled on the carcasses and had to be picked off before cooking began.

During this period bread was an important part of every meal – potatoes had not yet been introduced to England. Often the bread was cooked at a communal bakery, but most manor house kitchens had an oven, with a sturdy iron door, built as a big hollow in the brick-work of the wall. Several burning logs were placed inside and the door firmly shut. When the flames had died down the walls inside the oven were extremely hot. The bread, cakes and pies were quickly popped inside and before long the delicious smell of freshly baked bread was wafting about the kitchen. By the time the oven had cooled down, the food was cooked.

Food and drink

There were two meals each day. Dinner, served at 11
o'clock in the morning, and supper which was at four
o'clock in the afternoon. At dinner time the household
servants and the villagers who had been working on the
demesne came to the great hall, wiped their hands on
their tunics and sat down to eat at the long trestle tables.

Each place had a wooden platter, or possibly a slab of
bread which was used instead of a plate. The only cutlery
was spoons, and knives which people usually kept in
their belts. Fingers were used instead of forks and a
common sight was someone poking around a bowl of
stew looking for a tasty drumstick with the gravy right up
to his wrist.

The most important article on the table was a beautiful
gilt salt cellar. Tall and enamelled, it was a symbol of the
importance of some of the people seated at the table. The
lord, his family and guests sat 'above the salt', a clear sign
to the waiters as to who should have the choicest pieces of
meat, and the best wine which was drunk from thin horn
cups. 'Below the salt' was where the servants and villeins
sat – they were more likely to have soup made from left-
over scraps of meat, or bread and cheese, with homemade
ale drunk from tankards at every meal. Nobody drank
water – it was far too foul and muddy.

People very rarely ate fresh fruit or vegetables because
they believed this would give them wind. Plums, apples,
pears and cherries all grew in the village orchard, and
were stewed or preserved, rather than plucked straight
from the tree to eat. Sugar had to be imported from
abroad and was very expensive, so honey, carefully
gathered from the precious beehives kept in the village,
was used instead for sweetening puddings.

Table manners were appalling, people reached across
each other for food with grimy hands and tossed half-
chewed bones to the dogs who whimpered and slavered
by the tables. The straw on the floor soon became stinking
and sodden as ale and gravy was spilled and bones and
scraps left to rot. But in the Middle Ages people were
quite used to bad smells, for most of the household slept
on this filthy straw every night.

Fun and games

On dull, dark winter evenings merry games were played in the great hall. A young lad would pull his hood over his face and start a noisy game of blind man's bluff. Sometimes he even dared to catch the lady of the manor! Everyone joined in the fun, laughing and chasing each other around the hall, sometimes tripping over the barking dogs which scampered between the legs of the players.

Travellers were always welcome at the manor house, especially if they had an exciting tale to tell of adventures or wickedness in other villages. Minstrels were very popular, and often stayed for several days, or even weeks, entertaining the household with songs or music played on lutes or pipes which looked like recorders. Acrobats came too, and for a few nights' rest and plenty of food gave a magnificent display of handstands and cartwheels, tumbling and jumping at great speed to the gasps of the audience. Jugglers, who could toss half-a-dozen sticks into the air and then catch them one by one

before flinging them up again, kept their audience spellbound.

In the summer, when the evenings were lighter, hide-and-seek out of doors was good fun, or perhaps a wild game of football with no rules and an unlimited number of players. One of the great events of the year was the tournament held at the nearby castle. Here two armoured knights on horseback charged at each other with blunted lances and colourful shields, each trying to unseat his opponent, while the onlookers groaned with dismay or cheered with delight. Because so many brave knights were killed or seriously wounded in the tournaments it was decided that a low fence should be put between them. After this the sport became less popular because it was not nearly so exciting – all they could do was thrust and jab awkwardly at each other.

In a quiet corner, chess or draughts were played by the light of one of the few candles. Games such as backgammon, played with dice, were other favourites, though they sometimes ended with a lot of quarrelling if bets had been placed.

The lady of the manor

Travel in the Middle Ages was never easy. Roads were rutted and stony tracks, which were only suitable for travelling on horseback. Carts would either capsize into a pothole or break a wheel on one of the many rocks buried in the mud. Moving goods was so difficult that almost everything needed by the household had to be made at the manor itself.

It was the lady of the manor who made sure that enough meat, flour, honey, fruit, ale, wine, candles, medicines, and wool and linen for clothes was in store to last for the whole year. She was up at dawn to start organizing the servants – supervising a pig having its throat cut; showing a maid how to spin wool; making sure that the ale was being made correctly or instructing her cooks how to decorate a pie for a special guest. When her husband was assisting at the King's Court in the nearby town – or perhaps fighting in one of the many wars that were common at the time – she also supervised the work of the villeins on his behalf.

Spinning, weaving, sewing and embroidery were all done in the manor house. To keep out the cold wind, thick tapestries were hung on the bare walls of the solar and the hall. These were sometimes made by the ladies of the household who carefully wove coloured threads into intricate patterns of flowers and leaves, creating splendid hunting scenes or even a romantic knight bidding farewell to sorrowing maidens.

The Church and education

In the Middle Ages Catholicism was the only accepted religion, and even the smallest village had a church. The interiors were wonderfully decorated with glowing stained-glass windows and scenes from the Bible painted on the walls in red, blue and gold. There were no pews, but straw was spread over the floors. For the old or the sick, a few benches were set against the walls. The whole village had to attend church on Sundays and everyone was expected to kneel or stand throughout the service. On hot days it was not uncommon for people to faint, particularly when the sermon was very long.

Sunday was a day of rest, and anybody who disobeyed this rule was severely punished. Women who were foolish enough to do their washing on the Sabbath were publicly beaten however hard they pleaded to be forgiven because it had been a good drying day! The Church declared several days in each year to be 'holy days'. These became days of great celebration when feasts were held, fairs visited and people danced and sang till they were exhausted.

There was almost no education for the village children and even the daughters of the lord only learned domestic skills. However the boys of the manor were better off. The priest visited the manor house to teach them Latin. Later the lord's son might be sent to live at a baron's house as a page, where he would train to be a knight – or to a monastery if he wanted to become a monk. Sometimes he was sent to a grammar school where he learned Latin grammar and perhaps a little mathematics.

All books had to be hand-written. Most of them were written in Latin and kept in monastery libraries. They were beautifully copied by the monks with quill pens, although one Bishop is said to have complained about sticky finger marks on the pages. It was very rare for an ordinary household to have any books until printing was invented in the fifteenth century.

Parents were very strict with their children and believed that it was good for them to be beaten. Any rudeness was immediately punished with several strokes of a springy birch twig.

Clothes

Medieval people loved bright colours and often wore wonderfully clashing reds, oranges, yellows and blues. It was not uncommon to see a man wearing one red stocking with the other a brilliant yellow or perhaps deep blue. Nearly all the woollen and linen cloth woven in the village was coloured with dyes made of local plants, like bracken, lichen and even onion skins. Drab greens, saffron yellow or woad blue were easy colours to produce, but the dye for more exciting shades had to be bought from visiting travellers who sold powders made from crushed stones collected overseas.

Both men and women wore lots of layers of loose clothes, especially in the winter. A belted tunic over a woollen shirt and drawers was the usual outfit for a man or boy. For extra warmth they added a sleeveless surcoat which was like a long waistcoat, sometimes beautifully embroidered. On their heads they wore hoods which also covered their shoulders. Long hose kept their legs warm. These were not knitted but made out of cloth, tied with pieces of tape to stop them from slipping down and becoming wrinkled. Buttons were not used anywhere until later, when clothes were made to fit much more closely.

Women and girls wore a long gown, fastened at the waist with a belt, over a linen or woollen shift. Their arms were always kept covered, and a piece of cloth, called a veil, covered their hair.

Boots and shoes were made of strong linen or soft leather. They had very pointed toes but no heels. On wet days wooden clogs were tied to the bottoms of shoes to keep the wearer out of mud and to protect the thin fabric from becoming soggy and torn.

The Black Death

In 1346 strange stories came from the East of a terrible
plague that was killing nearly everyone who came into
contact with it. At first people in England were not very
worried about the news. China was very far away. But
later the stories became more frightening. The pestilence
was spreading across Europe at a fearful speed. In 1348 a
ship from France carrying the infection docked at a port in
Dorset. The Black Death had arrived in England.

The disease was carried from Asia by fleas which lived
in the fur of black rats. The first sign in humans was a
tickling nose, and it was that that spread the disease – one
hearty sneeze was all that was needed to scatter the germs
over a wide area. This stage was quickly followed by huge
swellings under the armpits which soon burst, and thick

yellow pus oozed and dribbled from the sores. But the fatal stage was when the body became covered in dark pustules, and once these had developed there was no hope. Death was agonising but very quick – in most cases people were healthy one day and four days later they were dead and buried.

Because knowledge of medicine was so primitive, people believed that a nosegay of sweet-smelling herbs would protect them from disease. A children's nursery rhyme is based on the Black Death: "Ring-a-ring of roses" (dark pustules), "a pocket of posies" (nosegay), "Atishoo! Atishoo!" (sneezing), "we all fall down" (dead!).

In three years one third of the people in England died from the Black Death and in many villages not a single person was left alive – not even the priest.

Although some villeins had been grumbling for years about having to work so hard on the lord's demesne, it was the Black Death that brought the quarrel into the open. So many people had died that it was not possible for those who were left to tend all the land using the old methods. Those who were already being paid wages demanded more money – those who were tied to the Feudal System began to insist on their freedom.

For a while, the lords tried to enforce the old system but the peasants gradually became angrier. A group of them, led by Wat Tyler, marched to London to demand justice from the King, but a knight pulled Tyler from his horse and killed him.

Although the revolt failed, the lords began to realise that the old ways were inefficient, and gradually feudal duties were lessened. When, in the Wars of the Roses, Henry Tudor defeated Richard III at the Battle of Bosworth Field, the feudal system had almost ceased. The villeins were free, able to rent their own land and work for a wage.